OLDEST BROTHER'S STORY

Tales of the Pwo Karen

by

Elizabeth Hinton

Photographs by Peter Hinton

SILKWORM BOOKS

Text © 1999 by Elizabeth Hinton
Photographs © 1969 by Peter Hinton

ISBN 974-7100-91-6

First published in 1999 by
Silkworm Books
54/1 Sridonchai Road, Chiang Mai 50100, Thailand.
E-mail: silkworm@pobox.com

Cover design by T. Jittidejarak
Set in 11 pt. Garamond and 9.5 pt. Helvetica

Printed by O.S. Printing House, Bangkok.

 CONTENTS

 PREFACE

This is a book about the Karen people—their stories and their way of life. It is based upon material I gathered late in the 1960s when my husband was involved in setting up the Chiang Mai Tribal Research Center (now Tribal Research Institute), North Thailand. The purpose of the center was to collect information on the various hill peoples on the borders of Thailand—the Hmong, Akha, Yao, Lisu, Lahu, and Karen. It fell to Peter's lot to study the Karen, and the Pwo Karen village he chose for study in 1968 and 1969 was Dong Luang.

To most people the Karen are a little-known ethnic minority of Burma and Thailand. If asked if they had heard of them, most—until recently—would have replied that they never had. But the Karen in Burma have been making world news lately as thousands have joined them in a protracted war with the Burmese government for their own independent state. With the fall of their jungle headquarters in Manerplaw in January 1995, they seem to have become yet another of the victims of the oppressive military junta that rules Burma. The villagers of Dong Luang, however, as residents of Thailand, have never been involved in the Karen war with the Burmese.

My interest in Dong Luang was in gathering Karen stories and folklore. In a society where people did not read or write, listen to the radio, or watch television, stories were of great importance. Stories entertained, transmitted history, taught right and wrong, and defined the Karen view of the world. I, too, found the stories of Dong Luang to be both entertaining and brimming with information about the

Karen way of life and world view. They were also touching human dramas—and literature in their own right.

The stories in this collection were recorded during evenings spent chatting by firelight, either in our own house or in the cosy intimacy of a Karen house, thatched to floor level for winter warmth. Most of the stories were told to us by Grandfather Pai, whose skill in storytelling was unsurpassed. Long Tuu was also a skilled storyteller and one of his stories appears, as well as those of two others. In the normal course of events, however, stories were told by anyone with a story to tell, whenever there were people to listen; so I have taken the liberty of setting these stories in the context of everyday life at Dong Luang, interwoven as it is through the events of the Karen agricultural year.

To translate the stories, I first recorded them on tape as they were told to me. Then I went through them slowly, phrase by phrase, often with the help of children who explained what they meant if I did not understand. Apart from a very little poetic license, I have rendered them as they were told.

Peter's photographs are included to complement both the stories and their everyday setting. Although many years have passed since these photographs were taken, I am happy to at last acknowledge the kindness, hospitality, and very real friendships that we enjoyed at Dong Luang.

Elizabeth Hinton
Sydney, 1995

ONE

THE KAREN OF DONG LUANG

A TALE OF GIANTS AND WITCHES

I shall always remember my first hours in Dong Luang. Deep in the mountains of northwest Thailand, not far from Burma, its cluster of thatched, split bamboo houses on stilts stepped down a dusty ridge to a small spring. The young men's laughing black eyes, sleek coiled hair, and tiger-cat tattoos were as striking as the dresses of the girls, which were heavily decorated with intriguing, red, fluffy, geometric designs.

The headman's wife blew up her fire when we arrived, so we could boil our billy of tea. Solicitous but unobtrusive, she made us welcome. That evening we were pressed to share several vegetable curries, one after the other, and then sat amongst a daunting gathering of curious young people, who took it in turns to pluck endless tunes from a teak banjo.

Weeks later, Somphop, our Thai colleague from the center, our cat, Nimmitibelle, some chickens, and the two of us, set up house in Dong Luang. The first disaster was the death of many village chickens from a disease brought by our lowland chickens. Then we got soap in the spring water. And every minute of the day we were subjected to scrutiny by fascinated villagers who addressed us in a language we did not understand.

The headman's eldest daughter, Uae Birng, loved to make fun of us. She would sit stiff and upright in our comfortable cane chair and mimic our feeble attempts to entertain, mouthing the sounds and words of Waltzing Matilda with great hilarity. Children would also visit for hours, drawing strange Karen designs with our colored pencils in the sun, chatting to us and teaching us their language as only children can.

Gradually, amidst the incredible strangeness, we found friends. There was Muu Mirng herself, wife of the headman. She had raised six beautiful children—including Uae Birng (White Rice), Yuay Birng (Abundant Rice), Pri Birng (Pretty Rice), and Gaw Birng (Rice)—and kept a watchful, motherly eye on us, presenting us with the fresh vegetables that were in season either in the forest or in her rice field: mushrooms, bamboo shoots, mustard greens, pumpkin, melon, yam.

There was Maang Diing Phaw, brother of Muu Mirng and the village priest. He was a versatile craftsman and we were to bring home with us a round, Karen, eating table which he had carved by hand from the base of a tree; also a Karen banjo, winnowing tray, and mortar. A widower, he came each afternoon for a cup of tea at the end of his day. Peter was his whisky-drinking companion during long nights of ritual drinking when no one else would last.

Cang, gentle and whimsical, was also a craftsman. When I told him that my father, too, loved making things out of wood, and also smoked a pipe, he presented me with a gift for him—a special lump of wood for a pipe.

Long Tuu, husband of Uae Birng, was a regular visitor, friend, and informant. One night we sat by his fire in secrecy and drank warmed wild honey out of his china whisky cups.

Diing Kang was the energetic, ambitious and visionary father of the elfin Mirng Mirng. When our much loved Nimmitibelle, the prized village rat catcher, was stolen by someone passing through, it was Diing Kang who organized a posse from Dong Luang to waylay the thief and rescue our puss.

Then there was Phii Birng, who could not contain her curiosity about the physical characteristics of an Australian female; and Sa Saw, fastidious, handsome, and full of dreams, who was so impressed with some hand-knitted maroon wool socks; there was Maw Saw, the village beau; his mother, Muu Lii, his aunt, Muu Naang; and Muu Naang Saa Tuu, outsider in the village and an excellent informant.

Lastly, there was Grandfather Pai, teller of tales. Grandfather Pai was happy to tell me some stories. I was curious to know whether they, too, had stories of giants and witches, like the giants and witches of my own childhood stories. Indeed they did, and he told me "The Giantess", a story set, like many others, in the days of old when the Karen lived in Burma and their lives were controlled by a hated Burmese overlord.

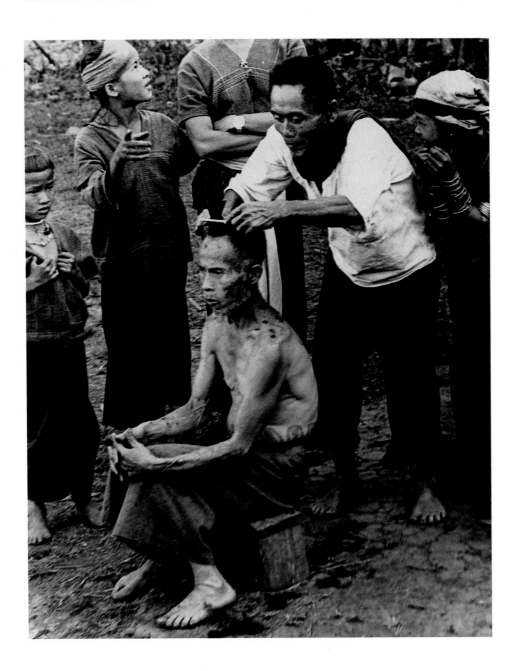

THE GIANTESS

This is the story of a poor orphan boy who lived alone in the forest with his grandmother because they had no other relatives anywhere. Every morning the orphan and the old lady walked down to the river to bathe. One day they met the children of the Burmese overlord. "Out of the way, Orphan! We are the children of the Burmese. Wait until we have finished!" The orphan was furious, but he said nothing and continued to scoop up the water in his gourd and pour it over himself.

"If you don't get out of the way, we shall push you out of the way!" The orphan quietly continued to bathe . . . Then push him they did—splash!—into the river.

As the orphan fell, he dropped his gourd water scoop and it floated quickly away on the current. By the time he had scrambled back onto the river bank it was around the corner and out of sight. Angry, unhappy, and dripping wet he rushed off to catch it.

The orphan ran quickly but there was no sign of the gourd. As he ran he came upon a woman enjoying the sun, right in the middle of his path. "Woman of the forest, did you notice a gourd water scoop floating by?"

"Indeed I did! I was busy brewing my rice whisky, or I would have gone and caught it."

"Many thanks," the orphan replied, encouraged. "Can I step over you, or would you prefer me to walk around?"

"It is polite to walk around." So he climbed carefully around the woman and continued on his way. "Bless you, boy, for your manners. May the giants have mercy on you!"

The orphan hurried on and not long after he came upon another woman. "Woman of the forest, did you see a gourd water scoop go floating by?"

"Indeed I did! I was holding my child out to excrete, or I would have gone and caught it."

"Thank you. Can I step over you or would you prefer me to walk around?"

"It is polite to walk around." So the orphan climbed carefully around the second woman. "Bless you, boy, for your manners. May the giants have mercy on you."

By now the river was growing broad and deep. Still there was no sign of the gourd. Then the boy rounded a bend. There, in the middle of the river, stood a huge woman! "This must be the giantess," he muttered to himself in fright, "inspecting her fish traps!"

"What luck! A juicy little human!" the giantess boomed in delight as she caught sight of the orphan moving on the bank.

"Don't eat me, Grandmother! I shall come and live with you as a grandson and keep you company!"

Now the thought of a grandchild appealed to the giantess, who was really quite lonely. "Very well, child," she said slowly. "Come and live with me and my old giant. But what brings you so far from home?"

"My gourd water scoop fell into the river and floated away on the current. I have been chasing after it, but I fear it is lost," said the orphan sadly.

"Oh, I found a gourd water scoop this morning. Come along home and I shall get it!"

So the orphan went home with the giantess. "Make yourself at home, boy," she said kindly as they entered her large house. "You can go anywhere you like, except on that shelf. But I shall have to hide you before the giant comes in, or he will gobble you up!"

The orphan peered around his new home curiously. The floor was of split bamboo, but the cracks between the slats were as wide as his leg. The kindling on the hearth consisted of great logs. And the door was so heavy he could neither open nor close it.

As soon as the giantess went outside, he climbed onto the forbidden shelf. Ugh! It was piled high with bones! Human bones! He broke out in a cold sweat. There were also two baskets on the shelf. One basket was old and worn. He lifted the lid nervously and peeped inside. It was brimming with gold and silver! The other basket was new. When he lifted the lid and peeped inside he found it was full of long grey pubic hair! Then he jumped quietly off the shelf again before the giantess could return.

"Boy! It's time to hide!" shouted the giantess as she hurried inside. "The giant will be home soon." She hid the orphan in a large cooking pot with a heavy lid, and not long after the giant strode in.

"Mmm! Something smells good!" he roared.

"What are you talking about?" replied the giantess.

But the giant knew there was a human in the house and he set about finding him. He looked over the fireplace, under the sleeping mats, in the rice pot. Finally the giantess said to him, "My husband, it's true there is a human in the house, but he has come to live with us as our grandchild. If you promise not to harm him, I shall let him out."

The giant gave his word and his wife lifted the lid of the cooking pot and helped the orphan to climb out.

The orphan lived with the giants happily for many weeks, fishing, hunting, and gathering berries from the forest. But, as time passed, he grew homesick for his old life with his grandmother in their little hut downstream. Eventually he said to the giantess, "Grandmother, I long to return to my own home. My human grandmother will be wondering what has happened to me."

"Of course, boy," said the giantess sadly, knowing she could not hold him against his will. That evening she came home with a wonderful catch of fish and crabs and frogs and prawns for dinner. She prepared them carefully and served them with vegetables and rice. They looked delicious.

The orphan helped himself to the crabs saying, "Grandmother, you and the giant have the frogs and prawns; the crabs are too hard for you to chew." He crunched on the crabs hungrily and ate his fill. "Thank you for a beautiful meal. Now what can I do for you before I return in the morning?"

"Boy, my head is so itchy. Would it be possible to sit in the sun and comb out my hair to kill the lice?"

"It would be a pleasure," he replied. At first light in the morning he went into the forest and searched until he found the poisonous root that killed lice. When he returned he combed out the giantess's hair and placed the root in it. Then he sat back and watched while all the lice ran to it, ate greedily, and dropped off dead. When all the lice were dead he said to the giantess, "That's done, Grandmother."

"So soon? Thank you, boy. Now you will need a basket for your journey. Which one would you like? The new one or the old one?"

"The old one will be fine, thank you."

The giantess reached for a basket from the shelf saying, "Off you go, then. But remember this: if the river is black, wash only your hair; if it is pink, wash only your lips; and wash only your face if it is really clear."

"I shall remember, Grandmother. Goodbye and thank you. I shall come and visit you again one day." Then he set off home, careful to wash only his face in the clear water, only his hair in the murky water, and only his lips in the pink water. His real grandmother was overjoyed to see him again. They were even more overjoyed when they opened the basket—the giantess had left all her silver in it!

News of the orphan's good fortune was quick to reach the ears of a young witch who thought to herself, "If the orphan can come home with all that silver, why shouldn't I?" So she, too, dropped a gourd into the river and set off after it. She, too, came across the woman who lived in the forest and asked if she had seen her gourd floating down the river.

"Indeed I did," replied the woman, "but I was busy and could not stop to catch it."

The witch muttered to herself impatiently, stepped over her, and hurried on without a word.

"Damn you for rudeness! May the giants show no mercy on you!" growled the woman.

At last the witch met up with the giantess and persuaded her, as the orphan had done, to take her home to live. Like the orphan she stayed for a time and then said she wished to return. Again the giantess prepared a delicious meal of frogs and prawns and crabs. But as the witch helped herself greedily to the prawns she said to the giants, "You have the little crabs. Although you are so large, your teeth are old and small."

"Rrrrr!" The giantess swore to herself, but she said nothing. After the meal she said to the witch, "Would you have time to kill the lice in my hair before you go?"

"I am in rather a hurry, but show me your head." She parted the giantess's hair and went over her scalp until she found some lice. "These are too big to be lice! They must be little scorpions!" And she took out her axe and chopped at her head to kill the lice. The giantess winced with pain at every blow and swore under her breath, but she still offered the witch a basket for the journey home. She chose the new one.

"Farewell, then," said the giantess, "but remember, if the river is black, wash only your hair; if it is pink, wash only your lips; and wash only your face if it is really clear."

Of course the witch paid no heed. She washed her face in muddy water and the silt stuck; she washed her hair in water pink with sediment, and it turned pink; her lips she washed in water that was clear and they lost all their color. She looked old and ugly. When she peeped into the basket for her prize, she found it was full of long, grey pubic hairs!

"Eeeeer!" she raged. She threw the basket away in disgust and made up a song about it:

The giantess I know, I know,
Is very well endowed
With pubic hair, with pubic hair!

The giantess heard about her singing the song. Full of fury, she stormed along and grabbed the witch, tore her limb from limb, and devoured her!

TWO

THE HOT SEASON—SOWING

TALES OF MAGIC AND THE SUPERNATURAL

When we first arrived at Dong Luang in late January, it was the end of the cool season and the beginning of the hot season—the time to prepare the year's new rice fields. Unlike lowlanders, who grow their rice in irrigated paddy fields, the Karen grow their rice in unirrigated fields, or swiddens, on the mountainsides. Each year they use a different swidden, rotating them carefully to conserve the soil. In return for intensive labor, swiddens provide good rice and vegetables for most of the year.

Long Tuu and Uae Birng had chosen to make a new swidden down by the river near the valley floor. Before we were even awake each morning they had left to climb down into the valley and spend the early coolness chopping down trees, dragging them into piles, and leaving them to dry out. They would then make their weary way back out of the valley and home.

After many sweaty, back-breaking hours, their job was done and they could rest while the chopped trees and branches dried out and the days and nights grew warmer.

Eventually a day was chosen by all the villagers as suitable for the "burn". It was chosen carefully as the success of the whole rice crop depended upon a good burn.

We watched nervously as Long Tuu set his field alight and the wall of flame and smoke roared up the hillside with terrifying power, engulfing everything in its path. But by evening the fire had died, leaving behind a blanket of thick, silver ash, rich in nutrient . . . Not a twig moved, not a bird sang, nothing disturbed the silent stillness . . . It was a successful burn.

After a small field hut had been built, Long Tuu was ready to sow his field with seed. On the day of the sowing there were many helpers. Amongst the group were Uae Birng's parents and all her younger sisters and brothers—cheeky Yuay Birng was there, with his hair, for once, neatly coiled in a sleek knot over one ear; and young Pri Birng, whose daily tasks were to fetch the water from the spring and to feed the pigs each evening. Uae Birng's regal cousin, Chii Duay, had come, and so had their friend Dae Birng, a serious fellow whose hair had been long and knotted some years already. Long Tuu's relatives were all far away.

The young men worked back and forth over the steep, ash-covered hillside, rhythmically jabbing their long dibbling poles into the hard earth and making holes for the rice seeds. As they passed on, the girls in their long white dresses followed after, deftly dropping a few rice seeds into each hole.

When every inch of the wide, steep slope had at last been dibbled and the holes filled with seed, people mopped their sweaty faces and sat down wearily for the welcome feast: first came the whisky drinking and the prayers to the spirits, and then the delicious pork stewed with rice and corn. After downing the whisky and the stew we felt pleasantly weary and tipsy and full. "Let's have a story, Long Tuu!" shouted Yuay Birng to his brother-in-law as he lay back on his elbow and filled his pipe with tobacco. "Let's have a story for dibbling your swidden!"

"What story would you like, Yuay?" Long Tuu's dark eyes smiled back as he, too, puffed contentedly on his pipe.

"A story of witches!"

"There are many stories of witches. I shall tell you a story called 'The Witch and the Python'."

THE WITCH AND THE PYTHON

There once lived a man who had seven lovely daughters, but none of them was married. One day he was out collecting firewood when he passed a tree laden with delicious fruit. A young man was in the tree already picking the fruit. "Hey there, brother! Could you fill a basket for me, too?" shouted the old man.

"Just toss me up your basket!"

So they shouted and chatted and the young man filled the basket. When it was full the young man climbed down from the tree to continue on his way but the older man stopped him. "Brother, you are a good man. I have seven lovely daughters at home and none of them is married. Could I present you to them as a prospective husband?"

"By all means," the young man replied, "but on one condition: that I appear to them in the form of a snake."

"As you will," the father agreed. Thereupon the young man turned into a python of shining gold and slid into the basket of fruit. The father closed the lid on him and carried the basket home.

"Eldest Daughter, I have something to ask you!" the father shouted as he entered his house. His daughters were below pounding rice.

"What is it, Father?"

"Do you want some berries?"

"Yes, please!" she replied climbing up the ladder to the house. "Are they really ripe?"

"The ripest ones are underneath." So Eldest Daughter put her hand into the fruit and pushed the top berries aside . . . only to find a snake, with its head waving and its glittering eyes fixed upon her! She withdrew her hand in fright. "How would you like that snake for a husband?" her father asked quietly.

"Why would I want a snake for a husband?"

So the father called his second daughter, and then his third, fourth, fifth, and sixth daughters in turn. All of them were repulsed and bewildered by the thought of a snake for a husband. Then the youngest daughter was called. As she pushed the top berries aside she, too, found the snake. "We're not going to eat that beautiful golden snake, are we?" she said.

"How would you like that snake for a husband, Youngest Daughter?"

"Would he be a good husband?"

"I think he would be an excellent husband, my child."

"Very well, then."

So a ceremony was held and, with a chicken and a bottle of wine for the spirits, Youngest Daughter's wrists were bound in marriage to the python.

As they went off together that night the python explained, "I cannot sleep with you in the house yet, little one, so I shall sleep in the bo tree near the temple."

Early next morning Youngest Daughter prepared her husband's breakfast and called him with this song:

Come and eat, my husband, come and eat;
Your breakfast is ready.

After breakfast, at his request, she rolled him a cheroot and prepared some betel nut to chew—though she wondered why a snake should want such things!

One morning the python told his wife to go down the river to wash her hair and bathe. So Youngest Daughter went into the forest and gathered fragrant herbs, which she boiled up to wash her hair in. Then she went downstream to bathe.

The python, meanwhile, had gone upstream to bathe. As he slipped into the cool water his old snake skin split open and sloughed off into the river and away. He himself emerged as a handsome young man, as dazzling as the glittering python.

When Youngest Daughter saw the snake skin floating downstream, she thought it was her husband being swept away on the current. So she grabbed at the skin and saved it; but it was rough and jagged and it cut her hand. Just then her husband appeared. "Thank you for trying to save me," he said gently, taking her cut hand in his and spitting healing betel juice onto it. Youngest Daughter was speechless with amazement.

One day Youngest Daughter and her husband returned to visit Youngest Daughter's father. "Ah, my child," he chuckled, "your sisters are all filled with envy!" They could not take their eyes off her handsome husband, especially when he took out his knife and ran it up and down his leg flaking off scales of pure gold! He collected a bag of gold flakes for each of Youngest Daughter's sisters to cheer them up.

News of the bags of gold traveled quickly and soon reached the ears of a greedy witch. Resolving to find such a husband for her own daughter, the witch caught a python, placed it in a large basket and covered it over with berries. Then she carried the basket home and persuaded her daughter to accept the snake as a husband. They were wedded that night and went off to sleep together in the house.

During the night the witch's daughter awoke in fright. "Help, Mother! My husband the snake is eating me! My foot is numb already."

"Don't be frightened, my child. Your husband is caressing you."

"Mother! He is up to my knee!"

"There is nothing to fear, my child. He is embracing you."

"Now he is up to my waist!"

The witch paid no heed to her daughter's cries for help; her thoughts were on bags of gold. Imagine her sobs when she discovered that all that remained to her was a great fat python asleep in the rafters!

Yuay Birng chuckled as he pictured the python consuming the witch's poor daughter. "Greedy old witch!"

"There are many witches in the stories of long ago," said Yuay Birng's father. "Did you know, Yuay, that it was because of a greedy witch that we now have to work so hard to grow rice to eat?

"Long ago, when the earth was new, the earth and the sky were joined by a long umbilical cord made of sticky rice cake. It was like a great pillar stretching up into the sky. No one had to clear fields to grow rice; they simply broke off enough rice cake to satisfy their hunger. There was plenty for everyone and everyone was happy.

"Then one day, along came a greedy witch. She stood beside the umbilical cord and ate and ate—all the way through the rice cake. Whoosh! Away went the sky, right up into the air where it is now. From that day men have had to work to grow rice to eat.

"At first there were no weeds, only bountiful harvests. One day, however, that same thoughtless witch was stumbling carelessly through the rice fields when she fell—bump!—onto a rice plant. The spirit was incensed by her clumsiness, so he made hundreds of weeds spring up amongst the rice. Now we must spend our time pulling up weeds and imploring the spirits for their help. Otherwise there will be no rice left to harvest."

"Lerh! Which spirit was offended, Father?"

"The Lord of the Land and Water, who protects us and watches over us. He owns all our territory and permits us to use it. We must always be careful to show him and his property respect, or he withdraws his blessing and we have famines and floods and many people die. That is why we must always obey his laws of right and wrong."

Pri Birng was listening intently. She was frightened of spirits. Only the other day a spirit had stolen one of her thirty-three souls, causing her eyes to be sore and itchy. She had had to offer it chicken meat, in exchange for her soul, before her eyes had recovered. Now, in a tiny voice, she asked: "Father, if we could see spirits, what would they look like?"

"Why, they are like us, Pri, and like us they all look different," her father replied. "Some are large, some small; some are beautiful, some plain."

"Will you tell us a story about spirits?" she whispered.

"I shall tell you a story about a spirit who had seven tongues, and who worried about himself just like we do! It is called 'The Orphan and the Spirit with Seven Tongues'."

THE ORPHAN AND THE SPIRIT WITH SEVEN TONGUES

There was once a boy whose parents both died at the same time, leaving him alone in the world. At first he just cried all day long and did not know what to do with himself; but after a time he took up his jungle knife and his divining bones and set out to make a new life for himself.

He walked for many days in search of suitable land near water—across rivers, up mountains, and down again into valleys. Then one day he came upon a huge house. The posts alone were six metres high!

The boy was fascinated and looked around for a way to climb into the house. Finding none, he took out his jungle knife and chopped steps into the nearest post—chop, chop, chop—and climbed up that way. There was a large rice pot on the hearth. When he could not reach the rice at the bottom of the pot he tied himself onto some rope and lowered himself down that way. He ate his fill, then pulled himself out again, and settled down to wait for the owner of the house to come home. He could not imagine who it might be.

Some hours later the owner came. He was a spirit. He was just like a person except that he was as tall as his house was huge, and he had seven tongues! He was delighted to see the boy. "La la la la laa! I went l-l-l-looking f-f-f-for f-f-f-food and c-c-c-came home empty handed; but here is a human d-d-d-delicacy. I won't g-g-g-go hungry after all!" he lisped and stuttered with his seven tongues.

The boy darted onto the hearth to run away. The spirit made a grab and the boy ran for his life. But the spirit soon caught him and dangled him by his balls: "La la la la laa! I'll ch-ch-ch-chop you into m-m-m-mincemeat!" he slathered.

The boy screamed. "We have only just met, and I haven't even spoken to you. Yet you say you will chop me into mincemeat!"

"Th-th-th-that's what I said!"

"Don't chop me up! Be my friend!"

"As if I would be your f-f-f-friend! I'd r-r-r-rather ch-ch-ch-chop you up!"

"In that case, I'll be your friend!"

"Well, if you are a g-g-g-good friend to me, I shall s-s-s-spare you," said the spirit, who was so self conscious of his stuttering tongues that he had no friends. "B-b-b-but if you are not a g-g-g-good f-f-f-friend, I shall just chop you up!"

"Oh, I'll be the best friend you ever had!"

The boy and the spirit lived together happily for a number of months. As more time passed, however, the boy grew restless. "I must continue my search for some really good land," he said. "When I have found it, I shall come back for you."

"I sh-sh-sh-should like that," said the spirit. "I no l-l-l-longer wish to l-l-l-live here alone."

So the boy continued on through the forest. One morning he came upon a strange sight: a huge old tree in the midst of a muddy clearing. When he looked more closely, he recognized animal tracks in the mud—prints of horses, elephants, cows—in fact, prints of almost every animal he knew. "Whatever is this about?" he murmured to himself. "I think I will stay around and find out, but I had better find a good hiding place."

He took out his divining bones and divined for a safe spot. He tested for each branch of the tree, but his chicken bones warned him that not one branch was safe. He divined for sheltering inside a hole in the trunk, and under the roots, and neither of these places was safe either. Finally he divined for inside the fork of a branch, and at last the bones indicated safety. So up he went, cut himself a hole and climbed in.

It was none too soon. Moments later, a huge spirit lurched out of the forest carrying a large sack on his back. "La la la la laa! I can smell someone here!" he sniffed. He climbed the tree, pulling off all the leaves. He lifted each root and peered beneath it. But there was no one to be found. "I can still smell someone," he muttered unhappily to himself, "but I suppose if they aren't here, they can't harm me."

The spirit sat down and untied his sack. Out trotted a horse! Then an elephant lumbered forth, followed by a cow! A Siamese man climbed out, and then the spirit brought out two beautiful girls whom he fondled lovingly. After a time he put them all back again, tied up the sack and lay down to sleep, with his head on the sack as a pillow.

High in the tree the boy used magic to lull the spirit into a deep sleep. When the boy tore off a large leaf and let it flutter down gently onto his face, the spirit did not stir. Nor did he waken when the boy tore off a small branch and dropped that onto him. Assured that it would be safe to leave, the boy divined again for the best direction to take. Then he climbed carefully down the tree, over to the spirit, and cleverly slipped a pillow of leaves under the spirit's head in place of the large sack. He picked up the sack and ran off as fast as he was able with such a heavy burden.

When he was a safe distance from the spirit, the boy peeped into the sack. As well as horses, elephants and cows, it contained all manner of things he had never seen in his life before: there was silver and gold, beautiful clothing, jewelry. It was no wonder the spirit flew into a blind panic when he awoke to find his sack gone! Desperately he cast a spell over the surrounding hills: they came down into his lap so he could peer into them for a glimpse of his lost treasure. He did it again, and again, until at last he caught sight of it! But, alas, it was beyond his territory and he was powerless to retrieve it. He stamped his feet in fury.

Meanwhile, the boy had tied up the sack again and slung it over his shoulder before continuing on his way. With new energy he scoured the hillsides for good land. But if there was flat land, there was no water; if there was plenty of water, the land was too steep. Just as he was despairing and planning to return to his spirit friend, he came upon his heart's desire: acres of gently undulating land in a saddle between ridge-tops, with a gushing stream in a nearby gully.

The very next day he took his knife and set to work clearing the trees—chop, chop, chop! He worked from dawn to dark everyday until he had cleared land for houses for himself and his friend and all his friends in the sack. At last he was finished. That night he went to sleep leaving his sack untied and in the morning he was surrounded by new friends.

The boy and his friends worked together then, and built a beautiful village. After that, they cleared land for their rice fields. And then it was time for the boy to fetch his old friend, the Spirit with Seven Tongues.

Back the boy went over the mountains on the long walk to his friend's house. Again he found the spirit's huge house empty. Again he climbed into the house, blew up the fire, and waited.

Towards evening the spirit came home. "L-l-l-lerh, boy, you have c-c-c-come back again!" he exclaimed with pleasure.

"Yes," the boy replied, "I have come back to fetch you." And he told his friend of his adventures, about finding the magical sack, about all the friends awaiting them in the beautiful new village, about the acres of undulating land, perfect for growing rice. The spirit was amazed at his story, and delighted at the thought of living in a village of friends, amid excellent land.

"I c-c-c-can't wait to see it all!" he exclaimed. "But f-f-f-first let me f-f-f-finish carrying in my rice, so we can t-t-t-take it with us."

"A good idea. I'll help you," the boy replied. Together they carried all the spirit's rice back to the house. Then they were ready to set out again.

Still the spirit seemed reluctant. "It's my s-s-s-speech," he finally admitted. "N-n-n-no one will understand me and they will p-p-p-poke f-f-f-fun at my s-s-s-seven t-t-t-tongues!" He could not be persuaded that it did not matter.

"Then cut off your tongues, leaving only one!" the boy suggested in desperation.

"What a g-g-g-good idea!" exclaimed the spirit and he hastened to fetch his knife. When he had cut off six tongues he found he spoke just like everyone else. He was thrilled. "Now I won't be embarrassed because I speak g-l-o g-l-a! Let's go!" he said triumphantly.

The spirit was amazed at the new village and the wonderful land and he and the boy quickly settled in. Indeed, it was not long before the boy had fallen in love with one of the beautiful girls, and the spirit had fallen in love with the other. They were all wedded and lived together happily for many years.

"Well that spirit was friendly enough!" Yuay Birng decided. "But thank goodness it's daytime. I wouldn't dare go home in the dark now!"

"Just remember that spirits have feelings and worries just like us, Yuay, and then they don't seem so frightening," said his father. "But it is time to go!"

Long Tuu and Uae Birng gathered up the dishes and spoons, packed the large cooking pots into baskets, and then they all set off on the long, hot climb out of the valley back to their homes.

 THREE

THE EARLY RAINS—WEEDING

TALES OF ORPHANS AND OVERLORDS

Not long after the last fields were sown, the rain poured down in torrents. The villagers watched anxiously lest their seeds be swept away. But the storms soon passed and gave way to lighter rain which the swiddens on the hillsides soaked up thirstily. Then the rice seeds began to sprout: the wet, black hillsides were dotted with tiny rice shoots of brilliant green. The weeds also sprang up in their thousands. Everyday, in the cool drizzle, people went out to cull them carefully from the rice shoots and young vegetables.

As the young rice grew taller, the villagers feasted the spirits imploring their protection of their crops. Baskets were woven to hold chickens which were offered to the spirits to feast upon; intricate shrines were constructed as shelters and resting places for the spirits when they had eaten their fill.

Because Long Tuu's swidden was cut in virgin forest, the weeds were few. This pleased Dae Birng and his friends when they visited, as their rests were longer here than where the weeds were thick. They worked away happily, singing out their songs of love across the valley, perfecting the words and melodies for hour upon hour, imagining themselves singing to a partner of their own.

But Dae Birng never joined in the singing. Eventually he muttered, "I am not handsome and the girls don't like me." And then it was clear why he never practiced the songs, nor had tiger cats tattooed on his thighs, nor wore glamorous bracelets or earrings or scarves.

"Oh, cheer up, Dae Birng!" Long Tuu reassured him. "There are more paths to a girl's heart than a handsome face! I can tell you a story about some poor orphan brothers who were favored by fortune and a girl because of their diligence."

So Dae Birng and his friends took their weeding knives and settled in the shelter of the field hut to rest, toast some maize to eat, and listen to Long Tuu's story.

THE CLEVER ORPHANS

Long ago there were two orphan brothers who were very poor. They lived with their grandmother in a tiny hut in the forest, far from the village. It was early in the new year and the brothers wished to begin work on a new rice field.

They visited the Burmese overlord to ask his permission, but when they explained where they wished to clear their field, the haughty Burmese sneered, "You poor orphans want to clear that rich land? Be off with you! That lump of rock yonder is suitable for orphans like you! Make your field on that!"

The brothers were angry and swore long and loud, but they had to obey the orders of the overlord. So, day after weary day, they carried great loads of soil and dead leaves up to the rock. Gradually they covered the rock with earth so rice seeds could be sown on it. And then they needed a field hut.

Again they had to approach the Burmese overlord—for permission to chop bamboo. Again he forbade them to chop it in the nearby groves of their choice and pointed instead to a distant mountaintop and told them to cut it out there.

Fuming with rage, the brothers rose before dawn next morning and set out for the distant mountain. By the time they were climbing the mountain the sun had risen in the sky and beads of sweat were trickling down their faces. When they reached the mountaintop the brothers sank thankfully back in the cool shade of the tall and graceful bamboos. Their eyes followed up the stems and into the sky. "What beautiful bamboo!" they exclaimed. "It's so clean and white and smooth! It won't even have to be cut at the joints!"

The younger brother scrambled to his feet and went further into the thicket. "Brother, come here! The bamboo is even more beautiful! It's a golden yellow!" he exclaimed in wonder.

Feeling cheered, they set to work happily chopping up their bamboo and singing as they worked. When they had finished they slid it, piece by piece, to the foot of the mountain. The white bamboo resounded like a silver drum as it crashed into the valley below; and the yellow resounded like a drum of gold. The brothers listened with delight to each crash, until all the bamboo was in the valley. Then they climbed down after it to collect it and carry it home.

When they reached the foot of the mountain, the bamboo was nowhere to be seen. Instead there were piles of silver and piles of gold. There was silver where the white bamboo had landed, and gold where the yellow had landed. The brothers recognized the silver, but gold they had never seen; they just stared in puzzlement. Eventually they thought to gather a little silver and a little gold to show their grandmother.

"My goodness!" she exclaimed when they had unwrapped their bundles. "You have real silver and real gold here! Is there any more?"

"Ever so much more!" they cried in excitement.

The next day they carried some bamboo home and built barns. The older brother filled his barn with the silver, and the younger filled his with the gold. They were wealthier than the Burmese overlord would ever be!

The brothers returned to working on their rice field. They built their field hut, and sowed the ground with seed. They went early each morning to carefully weed the seedlings as they grew.

It happened that the daughters of the Burmese also went early each morning to their rice field. And it happened that they had to pass through the orphans' field on the way to their own. One morning they came later than usual and met the orphans at work. "Good morning, daughters of the Burmese. Where are you going?" the brothers greeted them.

"We don't talk to shabby orphans!" they muttered, looking the other way and spitting as they went. They each spat as they walked past—except for the pretty youngest daughter, who thought the orphans looked rather pleasant. She stayed behind to talk to them.

"Youngest daughter of the Burmese, why are you late this morning?" the brothers asked.

"An old woman died last night," she said. "Her funeral will be held tomorrow night. Will you come singing with me, at her funeral?"

"But we can't sing!"

"I would be honored if you came!" She smiled as she went on her way.

"What do you think?" said the younger brother.

"We don't know a single song! How can we possibly go singing?"

"Brother, we could go home and get Grandmother to teach us some!" So they walked all the way home again and sat down to learn funeral songs with their grandmother.

She taught them all the songs she knew: songs to speed the soul of the dead to the after-world, songs in honor of parents, songs about a mother's choice of a suitor, boys' songs, girls' songs, courting songs, songs of modesty, songs of longing for a singing partner—every kind of song that was ever sung at a funeral! She taught them all night long. When the next day dawned she was still teaching them. Finally the old lady exclaimed, "Well, boys! That's all I know!"

Thereupon the brothers gathered some fragrant herbs, boiled them up, and washed their long black hair. Each one carefully oiled and combed it in a sleek, black knot over one ear, and added rings and necklaces, a green silk shirt, black trousers, and a studded leather belt. The older brother's knife had a silver handle, and the younger brother's had a handle of gold. Their betel boxes and pipes shone, too, with silver and gold.

"Will we do, Grandmother?"

"You'll do!" she replied happily.

When the brothers reached the village the funeral had begun. They joined the young men and girls in glittering singing capes and colorful clothes who were already circling the bier. Their voices rose loud and strong, speeding the dead woman's soul on its way to the after-world.

As the brothers moved round the bier, onlookers noticed their fine clothes and strong voices. "Those boys can sing! Whoever are they?" each one asked the other. Soon the whole village had come to listen to their singing. People forgot the children or grandchildren they should have been minding and watched, spellbound. "Their clothes are so fine! Their knives are of silver and gold! Whoever can they be?"

Then Youngest Daughter came along. "Hullo, orphan brothers!" she called out. "You came, after all!"

Youngest Daughter's father took her aside. "These are no orphans, silly! Where would orphans get such finery? I am the Burmese overlord, but even our things are not as fine as theirs!"

"But I was talking to them, yesterday! We know each other!" The Burmese overlord shrugged his shoulders in disbelief, muttering to himself, and went outside. And Youngest Daughter leaned over the hearth to blow up the fire and set about cooking a meal for the orphan brothers.

She cleaned the rice pot and washed the rice, then caught a young hen, slit its throat with her knife and singed its feathers in the fire. Having plucked it and chopped it into small pieces, she simmered it gently with herbs and spices. When the chicken was cooked and the rice was spread out on their round table, Youngest Daughter called, "Orphan brothers, come and eat!"

The brothers squatted around the table and ate hungrily. But before they could finish their meal, the villagers were calling, "Orphan brothers, come out and sing with the daughters of the Burmese overlord!" So they joined the other young men who were singing, bidding the girls to sing with them. When the boys had finished their song, the girls sang, bidding the boys, in turn, to come to them. After that, the brothers and the daughters of the Burmese went outside into the night, where they stayed until dawn!

As it grew light, they returned to sing again. But the girls were no match for the brothers. Youngest Daughter cooked breakfast, and while one brother ate, the other sang. They sang all that day, and the next night and day, and the villagers listened, rapt. Never in all their lives had the orphan brothers enjoyed themselves so much!

After three days and nights the boys were tired out and ready to go home. They collected their belongings, said their farewells, and set out. They had not gone far when, to their surprise, they came across Youngest Daughter sitting on the path, blocking their way.

"What are you doing here, Youngest Daughter?" they said.

"I wish to follow you home as your betrothed, Elder Orphan Brother!"

"But you will miss the funeral!"

"I don't care about that!"

"Go on," urged the younger brother, "give her your silk scarf!" He did, but that was not all. He also gave her his necklaces and pipe and knife! In fact, Youngest Daughter would not leave until he had given her all his possessions as a sign of their betrothal.

When the brothers told their grandmother what had happened, she was upset. "You went to sing, not to get yourselves into trouble! Now I shall have to go and sort out the mess."

And off she went to talk to the Burmese, to extricate her grandson from his unsuitable match. However the Burmese insisted that his daughter wished to marry the orphan brother and, after seven nights, he persuaded the old woman to permit it, too.

Some days after the wedding the Burmese visited his daughter and son-in-law in the forest. When he saw that they had three barns, he was curious. "Why ever do you need three?" he asked.

"Oh, the first is for our rice, the second for our silver, and the third for our gold!" the orphan brother replied nonchalantly.

The Burmese overlord thought he had heard wrong. But when he actually peered inside them, he was speechless with surprise. Eventually he managed to stutter, "Husband of my youngest daughter, it is not right that you should all live out here in the forest. You are only few; come back and live in my house until after the harvest, when you can build a new house in the village!"

So they did.

"Now tell us about the other paths to the hearts of girls," Dae Birng persisted. "What are they?"

"Another way to win a girl's affections is by using your wits. I know a story about an orphan who won the love of the beautiful daughter of the Burmese overlord in this way. It's called 'Fragrant Flower'."

FRAGRANT FLOWER

Long ago, in the World of the Dead, there lived a lovely spirit maiden called Fragrant Flower. Fragrant Flower was betrothed to be married to a handsome spirit youth, but she was dissatisfied. She wished to be born into the World of the Living. Her betrothed was impatient with her. "What makes you think you will be so happy in the World of the Living?" he exclaimed crossly.

"I just wish to go there and see it for myself," she replied. "I should like to stay until I am grown, but I promise to return to you before I marry." Nothing the boy could say would dissuade her, and she gathered together some friends to accompany her. One was fetching water but she stopped, saying she would finish when she returned. Another was chopping firewood, but she laid down her axe for when she came back. Yet another was weaving cloth, and another pounding rice. They, too, left their work unfinished saying they would complete it later. They all set out together for the World of the Living.

After many hours they reached the foot of the big bo tree, gateway to the World of the Living, where the Spirit of the Bo Tree ordained each human destiny. A Burmese overlord and his wife happened to be hiding among the twisted roots catching birds and they listened, fascinated, as the spirit maidens approached. "Where are you going, spirit maidens?" asked the Spirit of the Bo Tree.

"We wish to be born into the World of the Living and to stay a while," they replied.

When the spirit asked how long they wished to stay, the first replied, "A few months only, until I can roll over onto my side."

"Until I am old enough to fetch water," said the second.

"Until I can split firewood," said the third.

As for Fragrant Flower, "Until I am grown and young men desire me," was her reply. "But I wish to return to my betrothed in the World of the Dead before I marry."

The Burmese thought to himself, "What if she were to be born to us?" That afternoon he made love with his wife. "I believe we have conceived a child today," he said happily.

The months passed and a baby girl was born to the Burmese and his wife. They called her Fragrant Flower, because they knew that was her name.

It seemed no time at all before Fragrant Flower was grown. As word of her beauty spread, and the sons of the wealthy came to court her, her father began to worry. But the young men came in vain. Fragrant Flower, mindful of her vow in the World of the Dead, rebuffed them all.

Amongst her admirers was a young orphan. He did not dare to visit, however, for why would she be impressed by him when she was unimpressed by the sons of the wealthy? But the orphan's friend was shrewd and suggested a plan. As the last suitor was leaving one night, the orphan skipped up the ladder himself. "What are you doing here, orphan?" exclaimed the Burmese. "I don't want the sons of the wealthy, so why should I want you?"

"It's not your daughter, sire, but you yourself I have come to visit," the orphan replied. "Your daughter's suitors come riding on horses and elephants and they are trampling my rice into the ground. That's what I have come to tell you. I work hard in my field and I hope to have some rice to eat!"

"I can see your problem, boy, but I am not in a position to say anything. You must speak to them yourself."

To Fragrant Flower the orphan said, "Why do you dislike the young men? Many of them are both handsome and wealthy, yet you refuse them all alike."

"Ah, I do not wish to marry, orphan, because then I must return to the World of the Dead!"

"So that's the reason!" the orphan exclaimed with interest. Thoughtfully he continued, "What if your husband were to accompany you to the World of the Dead, persuade your spirit family to allow you longer in the World of the Living, and escort you back again?"

"What a wonderful idea!" cried Fragrant Flower. She ran off to tell her father about it. The Burmese was very interested in the orphan's suggestion.

"But no one would dare to travel to the World of the Dead and back," he sighed unhappily.

"I would," said the orphan quietly.

"Orphan," said the Burmese with tears in his eyes, "if you give your word that you will travel with Fragrant Flower to the World of the Dead, and persuade her family to allow her longer here, then she is yours!"

The orphan was overjoyed and ran off to tell his friend. Together they found a pig and some chickens and took them to the house for the marriage ceremony. Sure enough, before the feast was even prepared, the bride was ill. That evening she died. The orphan and his friend hastened to Fragrant Flower, erected candles at her head and feet, and instructed her mother to keep them alight to guide them safely back. Then they, too, lay down on either side of her and died.

The spirits of the orphan and his friend hastened to catch the spirit of Fragrant Flower. Before long they came upon her resting for the night, with friends from the World of the Dead who had come to accompany her home. When Fragrant Flower awoke next morning she looked at the orphan with surprise.

"Don't you remember, my beloved? We have come to accompany you back to the World of the Dead and to persuade your spirit family to allow you longer in the World of the Living."

"My friends from the World of the Dead are here now, so I don't need your company. Besides, I must keep my promise to my betrothed in the World of the Dead. Please leave us alone now, orphan."

The orphan was distraught to hear her talk like this. "How can she have changed so much? She agreed to my plan!" he despaired to his friend.

"Then we shall have to persuade her to agree to it again," his friend replied. "We shall follow at a safe distance and use magic to delay her progress."

So Fragrant Flower and her friends set out ahead of the orphan and continued their journey to the World of the Dead. Late that afternoon, due to the orphan's magic, they came upon a wide river, too deep to cross. "Let us wait here for the night," said Fragrant Flower. "Perhaps the orphan and his friend are still following and will be able to help us in the morning." To the orphan next morning she said, "I cannot marry you, my friend, but could you help us ford this river?"

Reluctantly they helped the spirit maidens cross the river, and they followed again at a safe distance. By nightfall distant rooftops in the World of the Dead were in view. "She is nearly home. You must do something quickly!" said the orphan's friend. The orphan blew magically on his hands again, transforming the maidens' path into a muddy quagmire.

"We can go no further!" Fragrant Flower exclaimed in frustration. "I wonder if the orphan and his friend are still following and could help us in the morning."

The next morning the orphan and his friend caught up with the spirit maidens while they were still sleeping. Gently the orphan woke his sweetheart saying, "Please, my beloved, request your family to allow you longer in the World of the Living. If I return alone, your honored father will kill me!"

Fragrant Flower was in a quandary. She was almost home, but could go no farther; and she had made conflicting promises in the World of the Dead and the World of the Living. She sat down to try to work it all out. Finally she picked up a large flat leaf upon which she scratched out a letter to her spirit father and she attached it to her pack horse to deliver it.

People recognized the horse when it galloped up to the village. "Ah, Fragrant Flower has returned!" they exclaimed. It was her father who found the letter.

"My husband from the World of the Living is following me home," he read. "He wishes to take me back to the World of the Living with him. What shall I do?"

"This young man must love my daughter very much," he thought to himself. "He must also be very courageous and clever." He wrote a letter in reply and sent it back with the horse.

"Orphan," said Fragrant Flower when she had read the letter, "my father says I should do as I wish. Please let us return to my father now."

"Very well," said the orphan sadly. "It is your decision." He blew upon his hands and the path became dry again; after that the journey was quickly completed.

Fragrant Flower was soon visited by her betrothed. When he saw the orphan and heard his story he was very angry. "I told you not to go to the World of the Living! Now look at the mess you're in!" he raged. That made the orphan angry, too, and he wanted to fight.

"May the best man win!" everyone agreed. "May the best man win!" First was the fight with bare fists, and a pig was killed for the occasion. The next morning was the fight with clubs, and an ox was killed. Both mornings the orphan sent the spirit youth reeling. On the third morning a buffalo was killed in honor of the duel with swords. The orphan slit his opponent's throat with one stroke.

So a ceremony was performed and Fragrant Flower and the orphan and his friend were restored to life in the World of the Living. "Next time you return to the World of the Dead, come together in old age," said Fragrant Flower's father.

Back in the World of the Living the Burmese was chiding his wife because she would not allow the bodies of the young people to be removed, although he had twice ordered that it be done. But she could tell that the bodies smelled fresher, as the young people drew closer. She called out for her husband to come and see for himself. "Wife!" he exclaimed. "You are a grown woman. How can you deceive yourself with such nonsense!" As she watched, however, she saw them begin to breathe. Gently she washed their faces and they opened their eyes and sat up.

There were great celebrations in the house of the Burmese that day. More pigs and chickens were fetched and Fragrant Flower and the orphan were married again, properly. This time they lived together happily until old age.

"But I have no wish to die for a girl!" Dae Birng cried, horrified.

"No, of course you haven't! But if you use your head, you will find the appropriate way to your girl's heart. It's not as far-fetched as you may think. We Karen have lots of orphan stories because we are like the orphans of the world: we are poor, we have no money and few possessions, and cannot even read and write. Even our land is not our own. It is only by using our wits and our skills that we are a match for the Thai or the Burmese or the Europeans, just as the orphans in the stories are a match for the wealthy and powerful overlord.

"When the Lord Buddha was creating humankind," Long Tuu continued, "he created people of all nationalities as brothers and sisters. We Karen were created first and were the oldest brother, and the Europeans were created last and were the youngest brother. The oldest and youngest brothers became great friends.

"To the oldest brother Lord Buddha gave ropes and knives and the knowledge of their use, and a betel box containing, among other things, writing. He was forbidden to open the box until he reached Burma, where Buddha had instructed him to live. To the youngest brother Buddha gave simply the gift of reading and writing, on white paper. He was told to go and live in the European countries. Buddha also gave all the brothers detailed instructions on how to live their lives, from the languages they should speak and the clothes they should wear, to the spirits they should placate, or the gods they should worship. Then the brothers all set out on their journeys to their homelands.

The Karen and the European, being friends, traveled part of the way together. The European brother was curious about the contents of his older brother's betel box but, remembering Buddha's instructions, the Karen brother refused to open it. "We are brothers and friends, and yet you refuse to show me what Buddha has given you!" the younger brother complained. Eventually the older brother weakened and they both peered into the betel box to discover its contents.

"The instant they raised the lid, the contents turned into a vast expanse of flat land—which they could neither put back into the box, nor carry with them! The poor older brother had to complete his journey without his land, without wealth and without literacy . . . and that is how he has been ever since. That is why the Karen are the orphans of the world and must live from swiddens cut on mountainsides belonging to other peoples.

"But don't be discouraged, Dae Birng! Because of our wits we are a match for the Burmese and the Thai and the Europeans. In fact, one day, our European brother will return to us and make up for the hardship he has caused us. One day we shall have a land of our own. One day you will find yourself a beautiful girl. And in the meantime, never underestimate the power of love itself!"

The young people weeded hard for some time after that, while clouds of mist and rain from the mountaintops swirled about them. At last their task was complete and they slipped and slithered on the muddy path to the shelter of the field hut. "Now, Long Tuu," they demanded, "you can tell us a story about the power of love itself!"

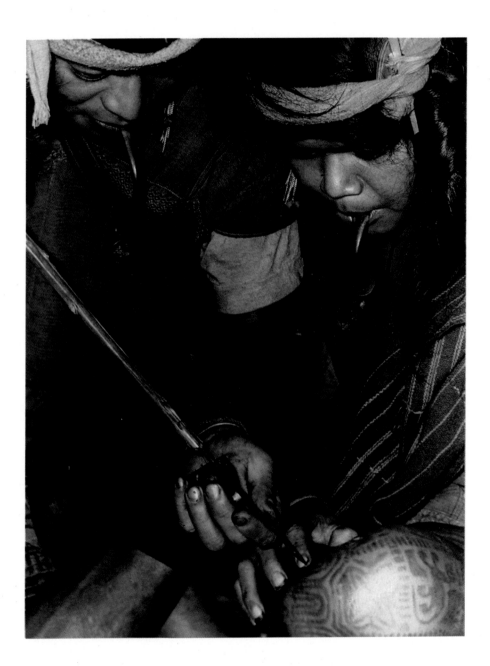

LAZYBONES

There was once an orphan who was very lazy. He was too lazy to even look for food. If mangoes were ripe, he would lie under a mango tree and let the fruit drop into his mouth. If it missed his mouth, he did not bother to eat it.

One day he was lying under a mango tree which was on the way to the rice field of the Burmese overlord. When the seven lovely daughters of the Burmese came along, they were cross. "Yyyng, Lazybones! What are you doing here? You are in our way!"

"I am having a rest."

"Well you shouldn't be having a rest on our path! We want to go to our rice field."

"Don't worry about me! Just step over!"

The first six daughters picked up their skirts, put their noses in the air, and hopped over Lazybones with disdain. The youngest daughter, however, hesitated, swinging her basket jauntily this way and that on her back. "Heh, Lazybones, what did you say? Did you say you were having a rest?"

"Yes, I am having a rest."

"Then which would you prefer? Should I just step over you, or should I walk around?"

"It's entirely up to you." But Youngest Daughter neither stepped over Lazybones, nor walked around him; she simply stayed and chatted.

Her sisters shouted back impatiently, "Hurry up, Youngest Daughter! We have a lot to do!" But Youngest Daughter still did not budge. Back they came to fetch her. "Yyyng! Youngest Daughter fancies Lazybones!" they cried in disgust. It was true. Youngest Daughter was thoroughly enjoying herself. She even sat down and shared her lunch with Lazybones while her sisters were busy weeding.

That afternoon Youngest Daughter's sisters hurried home in great indignation to tell their parents about her behavior. Her parents were upset. "You disgrace your family when you associate with Lazybones! You must promise not to talk to him again!"

But Youngest Daughter was very stubborn and refused to snub Lazybones. Indeed she saw him often and grew to be very fond of him. Her parents pleaded with her to give him up, to no avail. "Then we want nothing more to do with you!" they cried in anger. "Marry your Lazybones and your sisters will take you both downstream to where the ocean boils!"

At dawn the next morning the young couple's wrists were bound in marriage; then they were bundled into a boat, with baskets of rice, and rowed off downstream. As the sisters rowed, it grew hotter and hotter. The perspiration poured down their bodies and they grew weak with heat exhaustion, but they rowed on, waiting for the water to bubble and boil. Finally they could bear the heat no longer, so they cast Youngest Daughter and Lazybones adrift. "That will teach Youngest Daughter!" they said, as they rowed back upstream.

Lazybones gave his young wife a wink, for he and Youngest Daughter were clever and knew the ways of magic. As soon as their boat had drifted ashore, he bade her boil a little rice and water, which he offered to the spirits with this prayer:

"Spirits of my ancestors,
If I am indeed the husband of this young woman,
Grant that we be magically transported upstream again,
Three days' journey from my wife's family, to where it is cool."

Then they drifted off to sleep. During the night they awoke feeling cool. They were upstream again!

Thereupon Youngest Daughter used her magic. Swish! Swish! Swish! She slashed at the tall grass and cast a spell on it, saying:

"Turn into our companions,
Turn into our friends,
Turn into our houses and our land!"

Again they drifted off to sleep, and again they awoke to find the magic had worked: they found themselves in a beautiful village, with houses thatched with silver and gold, and filled with friends and companions. Lazybones and Youngest Daughter could not have been happier anywhere!

Years passed by and a son was born. He was a beautiful baby, but he was covered with sores. By divination the young parents learned that their child's suffering was caused by the soul of his grandmother. So his grandparents had to be fetched and a ceremony held.

Imagine the surprise of Youngest Daughter's parents when they saw Lazybones approaching their house. They were even more surprised to hear his story, but they reluctantly agreed to travel upstream for the ceremony.

Youngest Daughter was delighted to see her parents again. She happily let down her ladder of welcome with its rungs of silver, and laid out mats of woven gold for them to sit on. Her parents were dumbfounded. "Youngest Daughter," they gasped, "however have you acquired such riches? Your possessions are fit for a king!"

In fact they were mortified by her wealth. As soon as the ceremony was over they rushed back home and hung themselves!

Dae Birng was very impressed. "Perhaps I shall tattoo my thighs with tiger cats after all," he mused.

FOUR

THE MONSOON—WAITING

TALES OF SADNESS

The monsoon months persisted. Lush greenery appeared from nowhere all round the village; where there was no growth there was a sea of mud, churned up twice daily as the oxen went out to graze each morning and returned again at night.

The damp, muddy days were a time of hardship. As the rice became scarce, people mixed it with maize to make it last and they dreamed of the sunny months of plenty after the harvest, when the barns would be full of new rice.

These rainy months were also a time of illness. When a small child fell ill, her parents held ceremony after ceremony to different spirits, without success. One day she died. "It was time to return to her spirit parents," Pri Birng's mother explained. "Her mother told me how she pushed her aside and stretched her arms out to the door to her spirit mother who was calling her from the World of the Dead. When each of us is born, the Spirit of the Bo Tree asks us how long we wish to stay. Some say they wish to stay a short time only."

The unhappy parents held a small funeral for their child, and young people came from far and wide to sing around her bier and guide her soul on its way to the after-world. Chii Duay had persuaded Dae Birng, resplendent with tattoos, to be her singing partner!

Chii Duay and her friend were excited as they made their preparations. First of all they washed their hair in fragrant herbal water and carefully combed out the knots. When it was dry, they put on their very newest dresses, with ornate yokes and long red tassels. Then came the difficult task of arranging their hair in large flat mushrooms, anchored by dozens of shiny metal hairpins, but at last they had

set all the pins in place and wrapped the lot in silken scarves of brilliant green. That evening they powdered their faces, arranged their singing capes sparkling with beads and iridescent beetle wings, and attached long silken ribbons to their heads. They looked magnificent. Pri Birng was full of admiration as they went off to sing.

"It reminds me of the time when your father and I were young," Pri Birng's mother mused. "I first met your father at a funeral. I can still see his black eyes dancing with laughter as he sang to me, loud and true . . . Oh they were fun, those days! We sang together many times. You'll be out there one day, Pri, singing with all your heart to a handsome partner . . . New love is always born when someone dies . . . But now we must keep our friends company through their long, sad night."

There were a number of people in the cosy, firelit house playing cards, chatting, telling stories. The firelight flickered on the gnarled face of Grandfather Pai, disfigured by the scars of an old bear wound, as he recounted a sad story called "The Tiger".

THE TIGER

There once lived a man and a woman who had but one daughter and she was very dear to them. Every year as the rice was ripening the girl would sleep out in the field hut and guard the precious crop from the thieving animals and birds.

One year the girl was guarding the grain as usual when word reached the village that there were tigers around. It was just dusk so the girl's boyfriend lost no time in running to her field hut to warn her. "My friend," he panted, "there are tigers in the rice fields! You must come home with me at once!" But the girl was just settling down in the warmth of a cheerful fire and said, "Thanks, but I shall stay here for the night and come home in the morning."

"You must come now!"

"I shall come at first light tomorrow, I promise."

Nothing could persuade her to venture out into the cold evening air, so the boy went home again alone. "She is coming in the morning," he told her parents as he passed by their house.

That night the boy lay down to sleep but the thought of his friend alone in the field hut haunted him. For several hours he tossed and turned. Finally he threw off his blanket, took down his jungle knife, and sharpened it to a keen edge.

Slinging the knife over his shoulder he made his way back through the night to the girl's hut.

As he drew close he heard muffled screams and growls—the tigers had found his friend already! Cold with horror he drew out his knife, rushed into the hut and slashed into the tiger that was mauling his friend. But alas, his knife struck the girl as well. Both tiger and girl fell bleeding at his feet. In a few moments they were dead.

The boy threw himself to the ground in disbelief and his whole body shook with sobs. Of what use was life without his dear friend? How could he tell her parents that their child had been killed, and by his own hand?

After a time he grew calm as he thought of a plan which comforted him. Picking up his knife he deftly and lovingly divided his friend into three parts; then he cut the tiger also into three and laid it beside her. Taking with him three locks of the girl's long black hair, also the tiger's tail, he went back to the village. The tail, along with one lock of hair, he put into the mother's rice pounder; another lock of hair he laid on her winnowing tray, and the last he put into her rice basket. Then he climbed up onto his own house and, strumming his banjo, sang this song:

> *Mother of my beloved,*
> *Mother of my beloved,*
> *Go and see your child in the field, in the field,*
> *Your child in the field is not happy.*

The girl's mother was roused from her sleep by the song and strained her ears to listen. "That's a strange song he's singing," she said to her husband. "Listen."

> *Mother of my beloved,*
> *Mother of my beloved,*
> *Go and see your child in the field, in the field,*
> *Your child in the field is not happy.*

But they drifted off to sleep again and thought no more about it.

At first light the mother rose and went downstairs to husk the day's rice. As she took up her rice basket she noticed a lock of black hair in it. "That looks like my daughter's hair she said to herself in surprise. When she picked up her winnowing tray she found another lock of hair. Puzzled, she put her rice into the pounder and husked it. As she lifted the rice and the husks out onto the winnowing tray again she found herself holding the tiger's tail and the last lock of hair!

The woman screamed, threw down the tiger's tail and the winnowing tray and rushed up to her husband. "Our daughter has been taken by a tiger! Our daughter is dead!" she cried. Together they ran out to their field hut to see for themselves. Sure enough, they found their daughter in three pieces, beside a tiger cut into three. As they looked they understood everything the boy was telling them about her death: how she had been killed by his own knife as he had tried to save her from the tiger. They clung to each other and wept.

That afternoon the villagers took their axes and collected a lot of wood. They heaped it high and sadly laid the girl and the tiger on top and gathered round while the bodies burned. As for the boy, he was not among the villagers. He was at home, dressing. He put on his best black silk pants and shirt, fastened a belt round his waist and threw his beloved's singing cape over his shoulders. By the time he reached the cremation, the flames were licking high into the air.

The boy stood by the fire and looked into the dazzling heat. In its depths he could make out the shape of the tiger chasing his friend, and drawing closer and closer to her! He quickly grabbed his knife and thrust it into the fire, stabbing deep into the tiger's heart. He stood for a moment in silent exultation, then he leapt triumphantly into the fire to his beloved!

Pri Birng put her head in her mother's lap and, listening to the rain falling softly on the thatch, the singing from under the house, and the snatches of conversation in the room, fell fast asleep.

The morning after the funeral, the girl's body was carried from the house to the knoll of the dead where it was buried. The forest was dripping with rain and the wood was too wet to burn. A little shelter was made for the child's spirit to rest in and gather strength for the long journey back to the World of the Dead. And her favorite belongings were left for her to take with her on the journey.

Pri Birng and her mother slept at their friend's house again that night. The family was frightened of their dead child's spirit and the illness it could inflict upon them. Perhaps it would return to the house to collect more belongings, or because it would meet difficulties on the long journey to the World of the Dead. Everyone sat close for comfort and fell silent, spines tingling when the dogs barked. It was near midnight before someone thought to ask Grandfather Pai for another story.

THE FLOWERS OF THE MUSTARD GREENS

Long ago there was a young orphan who owned seven oxen, seven dogs, and was betrothed to a beautiful young maiden. The maiden wished to be married without delay but the orphan said, "I have neither drum nor riches yet. I must go trading for a year or two to make my fortune." He promised to be back by the third year at the latest. "Please wait for me and be worthy of my trust."

The very next day he prepared a large bundle of betel nut and a stack of cheroots; then he harnessed up his seven oxen and set a pair of bells on each one's back. When his seven dogs and seven companions were ready he bade farewell to his betrothed and set out.

The path wound down in front of the village into the valley, then up again and round behind the mountainside. Hours later the boy could see his girl's house far off across the valley; and the girl could hear the ox bells ringing out to her in the distance. She ran to look, untied her red scarf and waved to her boy. The ox bells sang back:

> *We shall return bearing silver and gold;*
> *We shall return bearing silver and gold.*

By noon the boy, along with his oxen, dogs, and companions, had disappeared from view and the girl was left lonely and forlorn. She shed some tears and could not eat.

A year passed by. The girl's father, who had never liked the orphan, grew impatient for his daughter to be married. He brought eligible suitors to her in fine clothes and said, "What do you think of this man? He owns a horse, an elephant, and a drum!"

She would reply, "Father, I am waiting for my betrothed."

"A whole year has gone by and you have heard nothing. He will never return now."

"He promised to be back by the third year at the latest!" she would retort angrily.

Another year passed. The orphan was still faraway but he had completed his business and was returning. The homeward journey was long and slow as there were mountains to climb and rivers to cross. "Your boy would be home by now if he were coming," said the girl's father. "He must have perished along the way." He had selected another husband for his daughter, a man from a distant village with three hundred silver coins. Even her mother agreed that it was an excellent match. The girl refused to discuss the matter, but preparations were nevertheless made for the wedding. When she asked her parents what they were doing, they replied, "Your boy has been gone too long. He won't return now, he must be dead." They would not wait and set about distilling the rice whisky.

Meanwhile the orphan was drawing closer everyday. People in the village where he was staying said to him, "You will be home in time for a wedding."

"Oh? Who is to be married?"

They told him his girl's name. "She is marrying a wealthy man from a distant village." The boy's heart sank. He could no longer eat. The food just sat in his throat.

"She promised to wait for me," he repeated to himself, over and over again.

"Hurry back and you will be in time for the whisky drinking!" But the boy had no thought for whisky now. In fact he had lost all desire to even return. Eventually, though, he forced himself to harness up his oxen and trudge homewards, leaden hearted. He bought the wedding gifts he would have given his bride—red and black cotton thread of the best quality—and finally stopped to rest at another village.

"You will be just in time for the wedding feast!" they said. "There are two nights before the pig will be killed and if you hurry you will be in time to have some." But the orphan was in no hurry and stayed till morning. Then he harnessed up his oxen again and traveled through the day. By evening he was tired and hungry and angry. His companions prepared a meal, but he could swallow only a few mouthfuls. Although he lay down to rest he was too unhappy to sleep.

He tossed and turned fitfully until, in desperation, he called out to his companions, "Let's get going!" So they harnessed the animals up again and traveled through the rest of the night. By dawn they could see their village across the valley and hear the gongs and cymbals welcoming the groom.

As for the bride, she had not yet risen. She lay in her blanket, still and sad. Then, floating across the valley came the sound of ox bells! "My boy is back!" her heart shouted and she could no longer lie still. His music was drawing closer and closer—it was beautiful! The bells sang out:

We are bearing drums and riches;
We are bearing drums and riches.

Now they were descending into the valley. How long had it been since she had put up her hair and made herself beautiful? She grabbed her oil and carefully arranged her hair, then tied on her green silk scarf. She could see her boy through the slats in the bamboo walls of the house—his arms and legs, his silver-handled knife and his skin bag. Her boy had come home to her at last!

Pretending to need water, she took up her bamboo water containers and ran down to the stream to meet him. She scooped up water, and scooped up water, until at last he came. "Oh, it's you!" he said and continued on his way. Then he shouted back over his shoulder, "I thought you were going to wait for me and be worthy of my trust! How can you be marrying another?"

"My beloved, it's not my doing! It's my father!"

"If you don't wish to marry the man, how can he want you?"

"If you don't believe me, ask anyone!"

"So you do still love me?"

"I shall love only you until the day I die!"

The orphan paused, then he said slowly, "If that is the case, can you agree to this?" And he told her and his companions of his plan. His girl replied that she would agree to anything—that she did not love the bridegroom at all. And his seven companions solemnly nodded their agreement. "Then come and fetch me when my mustard greens are in flower." At that, the orphan drew out his long, sharp, silver hairpin and plunged it into her body, just beneath her breast, and left it there. "If you can reach your house," he said, "lie down on your sleeping mat."

The girl picked up her water containers, put them on her back, then climbed slowly back up to her house. She said to her mother, "Could you please unroll my mat. I am still sleepy." So her mother unrolled her mat. "And could you bring me my two silver cups. I wish to drink from them." Her mother brought her the cups and went away again to chat.

When the girl was alone she carefully pulled out the hairpin, then pressed her silver cup over the wound. She lay down on the cup and her life blood dripped slowly into it.

Her mother had no idea what had happened. When some young friends called by, she exclaimed impatiently, "My daughter, you are still sleeping and your friends are visiting! Why, you haven't even let the chickens out yet!" She went over to shake her daughter to rouse her. It was then she saw the blood. She tore off the blanket and there was her child, dead.

The news soon reached the groom and when he saw that she was indeed dead, he shrugged, slung his drum over his shoulder and set off home again without even waiting for the funeral. In fact he only left the pigs and chickens he had brought for the feast because he did not want to carry them; those with an appetite ate them.

The girl's parents were beside themselves with sorrow, but the villagers muttered to themselves that it was they who were to blame. They had forced her to marry against her wishes; and had not her betrothed returned that very morning, laden with riches, before the two years had long passed?

For three days and nights people gathered to sing the girl's spirit back to the World of the Dead. For three days and nights the orphan watched and listened. Then, as planned, he harnessed up his oxen for the last time and led them out into the fields where he killed them, one by one, and chopped them into meat for the villagers. One by one, as planned, he also killed his seven companions.

A huge pile of firewood was collected, and the bodies of the girl and the seven companions were laid upon it. The boy also laid upon it the red and black cotton thread, some of the girl's belongings, and some clothing of his own. The fire was lit and the flames towered to the sky burning everything up. At last there remained only glowing embers. As the villagers stood watching they listened in amazement. Bells could be heard faintly ringing—ox bells! The orphan's companions were leading the girl and the oxen back to the World of the Dead and she was laughing as she went. The orphan listened, rapt, until the sounds faded into silence and the embers collapsed into ash.

The orphan did not build himself a house in the village but lived in a rough hut on his field. He dug himself a small vegetable garden and sowed it with mustard greens. He thought constantly of his betrothed. One night he dreamed of her and said, "I am so alone. Why have you not come to fetch me?"

"Because your mustard greens are not yet in flower," she replied.

The orphan waited. He had no rice, so he hunted for deer and wild pig and exchanged their meat for rice. Everyday he longed for his beloved. Then one day, as he was weeding his vegetables, he noticed clumps of yellow on them. His mustard greens were in flower at last!

The orphan hurried back to his hut and sharpened his spear. When the point was as fine as he could make it, he called his dogs to go hunting. The dogs soon picked up the scent of a wild elephant. Skillfully they tracked it, leading him quietly to it. The orphan sized up the elephant, took careful aim, and speared it—through the head from behind and out the other side. The elephant, mad with pain, charged at the orphan with its head lowered. The spear from its head caught the orphan beneath the heart and blood gushed freely from the wound. The orphan soon collapsed and died.

When the villagers saw what had happened they nodded their heads in understanding, saying, "Ah, the mustard greens are in flower; he has gone looking for his beloved."

They took up their axes sadly and chopped enough wood to burn him. But he would not burn. So they killed his dogs, too. Then the fire burned.

As they burned, the dead came to meet them. People saw the girl, laughter and welcome on her lips, the seven companions, and the seven oxen with bells chiming gaily, leading the orphan into the World of the Dead. They watched in fascination until they passed out of sight and could be seen and heard no more.

The next night Pri Birng and her mother returned home to sleep soundly. Chii Duay was home again, too, and fast asleep. She and Dae Birng had had an exciting funeral.

FIVE

THE COOL SEASON—HARVESTING
TALES OF LOVE AND LAUGHTER

As the weeks passed the steady rain gradually eased, the thick low clouds dispersed, and the sun shone. The world was new again. The slippery, oozy mud thickened, then dried into hard holes that tripped the unwary. The girls picked garlands of frangipani and marigold for their hair.

The fat green grains of rice grew gold in the sunshine, and the people knew they were ready to be reaped. Each morning before light, and again in the evening, the rich, mellow tones of the harvest horn echoed joyfully across the valleys as the villagers went out to harvest their rice.

The young people enjoyed the harvest. They went out in their groups to help each other's family with their crop. Each boy had a girl to whom he passed a fistful of rice stalks as he cut them off; then the girl bound the stalks into bundles and laid them gently down in stooks.

Yuay Birng, Chii Duay, Dae Birng, and their friends visited Long Tuu's swidden for a day. It was barely light as they skipped down the track through the forest. As the long fingers of dawn reached into the valley, they came upon the rice field: a hillside carpeted with gold. Long Tuu was very proud; his fondest hopes for a fine crop had been fulfilled.

The young people wasted no time in taking out their reaping knives and finding partners, as harvest days were long and busy. They reaped and bound up the bundles of rice all through the day, stopping only for quick snacks of rice and chillies, or perhaps a slice of melon from one of the vines in the field.

Yuay Birng loved to tease Chii Duay and Dae Birng. "Look at the sweethearts, Long Tuu," he whispered. "See how they have eyes only for each other?"

Only when the shadows were growing long again and the light was fading did they put down their reaping knives and survey the large section of the swidden they had shorn that day. Weary but happy, they made their way home in the growing darkness, ready to swallow some dinner and collapse in sleep.

When each family's rice had been reaped and laid out to dry in stooks, the loose, dry grain was carefully threshed from the stalks. Then it was carefully fanned to blow away the chaff and bits of stalk or dry leaves, and stored in the field huts. This was a time of anxiety for the villagers, as they guarded the product of their year's labor from thieves, animals, and even spirits, whom they placated in a variety of ceremonies with delicious feasts. It remained to carry the rice home to the village to be stored in the barns—and the year's work was again complete.

The days were sunny and the evenings cool. People loved to sit out on their verandahs to chat or watch the dusk draw in over the mountains. They would gather in groups to gossip. They would scrape some sticks together for a small fire and stand or squat as they listened. Long Tuu told these stories about cousins for Yuay Birng and the "sweethearts of the harvest"!

THE COUSINS

There once lived two sisters whose husbands had died. The older sister had a son, and the younger had a daughter. When the older sister also died, the younger woman looked after both the children as if they were her own. She would say to them, "Now you behave yourselves, or I'll send you straight back where you came from!"

The two cousins were as brother and sister to each other and went everywhere together. One day, however, the girl decided to stay home to thread her loom and weave some cloth. "Cousin, can you go to our neighbor's field without me, today?" she said. "I wish to stay home and weave." But the neighbors were troublemakers. Noticing that the boy came alone to their rice field, they were quick to gossip behind his cousin's back:

"She says dreadful things about you!" they said. "How can you bear to live with her?"

"Troublemakers!" the boy said to himself, and took no notice.

The next day his aunt sent him to chop bamboo posts for their barn and it was his cousin who went alone to the neighbor's rice field. "How can you live with him when he says such terrible things about you?" they said. She was hurt and angry.

"How could he say such things?" she muttered. "I'll teach him!" So she ran home, cooked the dinner, and ate it all before her cousin came home. Then she went out to visit a friend.

"Where is my cousin?" the boy asked as he scraped the mud from his feet and stooped to pass beneath the low entrance of the house.

"I'm not sure," his aunt replied. She was here a minute ago." She called to her daughter to come and cook some dinner, but there was no reply and the boy had to cook his own. He was upset then.

"Why is she behaving like this?" he said to himself. "I took no notice of the lies they told me about her!" He knew they must have said similar things to her. As he stirred his rice the tears trickled down his face into his dinner. "How could she believe them?" he thought.

It was the same the next day. The girl rose before dawn, packed her own lunch and left before her cousin was awake. His aunt packed his lunch for him saying, "There was no bundle of rice for you today." Lonely and unhappy he went off to chop the posts for the barn. He was miserable all day and worked especially hard so as to forget the bitterness within him. By late afternoon he was almost finished. There was just one more post left to chop, when—slash—he caught his wrist instead of the bamboo! Blood spurted in all directions!

One drop flew high and far, landing on his cousin working in the rice field nearby. She put her hand on her heart and found a large, round drop of blood. "It is my cousin's, I know," she said fearfully.

Meanwhile her cousin managed to stagger home, blood pouring from his wrist. Weak from shock and loss of blood, he sank at his aunt's feet and gasped, "They gossiped and lied to me about my cousin the other day, but I didn't believe them. When she came home from the fields she was angry and ate my rice and drank my water. She betrayed my trust!" Then he died.

The headman beat the drum of death. People heard it and came hurrying home from the fields. The boy's cousin came, too. She saw the trail of blood. When she was halfway home a child told her, "It's your cousin—he's dead." She rushed home, threw herself on his body, and sobbed.

Her mother said, "Your cousin said that people gossipped to him about you, but he took no notice. You believed their lies about him and ate his rice and drank his water. He died feeling you had betrayed his trust. He was very dear to me. And now who will go with you to the fields?" Her daughter was distraught with grief and remorse.

A funeral was held for the boy and people came and sang songs for him. After three days and nights they burned his body on his field. His cousin could neither eat nor drink and wished only that she could die.

As it was harvest time, the girl's mother went alone the next day to reap the rice. All day long she reaped, and all day long she thought of her nephew and wept for him. By dusk she could do no more and prepared to leave. "Aunt," said a voice in the shadows. She spun around in fright. "Don't be afraid, Aunt, it's only me," said the voice.

"You sound like my nephew, but he is dead!" she exclaimed. "We burned him on this field just yesterday!"

"I am your nephew. Can you stay and talk a moment?" Of course the woman stayed and talked with her nephew's ghost. She told him how they were missing him and how her daughter would neither eat nor drink and wished to die. "Please tell my cousin," he replied, "that if her heart is still with me, she can come and harvest with me tomorrow. As my death was by accident, I am barred from the World of the Dead and must remain here on my field. It would give me pleasure to join her in our harvest."

The girl needed no second bidding and went next day to harvest. She was overjoyed to be joined by her cousin's ghost. They worked together and talked together happily all day. As evening fell, the other helpers went home and only the girl was left with the ghost of her cousin. She was not afraid. He said to her, "Your friends have all gone home. It is time for you to go as well."

"I would rather stay with you."

"But your home is in the village."

"I shall not go home unless you come, too."

"You know I cannot do that. My home is here now. Unless, of course, you care enough and are brave enough to venture into my home up there among the ghosts, to collect my belongings?"

"I would do anything to have you back again!" Trembling from head to toe the girl crept up among the ghosts of the dead, to where her cousin had been burned, and fetched the bag and mouth organ which had been burned with him. Then she fled back to her cousin, and together they walked back to the village!

As they walked, the boy played all the old tunes he used to play on his mouth organ. People heard them and thought to themselves, "That sounds like our friend, but he is dead."

The girl went home to her mother and said triumphantly, "Well, here we are, Mother!" Not long after, a wedding ceremony was held, and the girl and her cousin had their wrists bound in marriage.

MORE COUSINS

There once lived two brothers. They were handsome and popular and enjoyed life. They sang at funerals, and dressed in fine clothes and beautiful jewelry they fashioned themselves; and each year after the harvest they set out for distant villages in search of adventure. The last thing they wanted was to marry and settle down.

But, one by one, their friends married and had children. As the years passed by, the brothers knew that they, too, would have to marry soon or remain bachelors forever. So the older brother found himself a wife.

Three years later, however, the couple were still childless. The younger brother realized that he, too, had no time to waste and found himself a wife as well. Strangely, both women soon became pregnant. Even more strangely, nine months later they both went into labor on the same night. The brothers met on the path as they each went to hang their child's umbilical cord in a tree to dry; one brother had a son, and the other had a daughter.

The children were perfect companions and quickly became inseparable. At first the brothers were happy about this but as the years passed they grew uneasy. "It's not good for the children of brothers to be so close," they agreed. After much discussion it was decided that the older brother would take his wife and daughter and move to a distant village.

More years passed by and in no time at all the younger brother's son was ready to look for a wife. But, to his father's dismay, he refused. "If I cannot marry my cousin, then I shall remain a bachelor," he said. He was adamant.

Eventually his father relented. "If that is how you feel, then you had better go and find her!" So the young man gathered together some friends, and some bags of rice, chillies, and salt, and rowed down the river in search of his cousin.

He inquired at every village, but the reply was always the same: "We have not heard of her," they said, as they shook their heads, unable to help. When the food was all eaten, they had to return home.

The father was sorry, but not surprised, to see his son come home alone. He knew from the travels of his own youth how many villages lay scattered through the hills. Nevertheless, he understood his son's longing. "Perhaps you should look among her spirit relatives next time," he suggested.

More food was packed and the young man and his friends set out a second time. They had not been traveling long when they happened upon an old woman who lived in the forest with an orphan. She listened carefully to their story and replied, "Your cousin does indeed live in that village yonder. But she is betrothed to a young man there."

The young man's heart turned over. "But I want to marry her myself! She belongs with me!" his thoughts shouted. Out aloud he said to the old woman, "May we stay here and help you with your rice field? I can see you have few hands and much work."

"By all means," the old woman agreed, pleased at the prospect of help and companionship.

So the young man stayed and helped the old woman and the orphan to clear their rice field. He climbed the trees and lopped the branches as he had always done at home, while his companions cleared out the undergrowth. When the field had been burned, they helped to build the field hut and to sow the field with seed. As the rice plants grew they kept them weeded until the time came when they could sit back and wait for the grain to ripen ready for the harvest; ready for the day when everyone would come from the village to help the orphan to harvest his crop.

At last the day came. The young man rose before cock crow. After eating his breakfast he hid himself in a far corner of the orphan's field where the ground sloped out of sight, and waited. Sure enough, at dawn his cousin appeared. She was with her betrothed and happily playing her mouth organ. They began to harvest; he reaped the ripe stalks carefully, while she bound them up for him. Her red bag hung over her shoulder and if he wished to smoke, she took tobacco from her bag and filled his pipe for him; if he wished to chew betel, she prepared that for him, too. When they were hungry they went down to the field hut and ate. It was then that the girl looked up and saw how the trees had been lopped.

"Someone has lopped the trees!" she said to herself in surprise. "Someone has lopped the trees just like my cousin used to do at home!" She finished her food in silence. Then she handed her tobacco bag to her boy, saying, "You take care of this now; I want to go into the forest." When she was amongst the trees she chose a tall one, pulled up her dress, and climbed up the trunk. She balanced carefully along a branch and scanned the field for some sign of her cousin, but there was none. She climbed along another branch which gave a good view in a different direction, and looked again. This time she saw a lone figure in a far corner harvesting rice. She scrambled down the tree and ran over to him. They both gasped with pleasure at seeing each other again. She placed her hand on his arm saying, "My cousin, when did you come? Why have I not seen you before?"

"Why would I see you? You are betrothed to be married."

"But I didn't know you were here! Can I tie up your rice bundles for you?"

"You'd better not." But he stopped his work and took her hand in his. After that she just picked up his rice bundles and bound them up for him. She no longer even thought about anyone else.

The hours passed by and they scarcely noticed the sun go down. But it was then that her boyfriend really missed her. "Why ever hasn't she come back?" he wondered with concern. "She only went into the forest!"

"Oh, I saw her tying up rice with someone yonder!"

At that her boyfriend's concern turned to anger. He pulled out his knife and flung it onto the ground. He grabbed it up again and hurled it into a tree. He was furious. Meanwhile the cousins were still happily reaping.

As the shadows grew longer the girl said, "It's time to go home. You must come, too."

"But your boyfriend will be very angry by now. You can't possibly go home!"

"If he's angry, he's angry. He'll kill us! But we can only die once! Let's go."

When the cousins arrived back at the village the boy was still raging. "Come and fight!" he yelled when the cousins appeared. "I want to stab you to death, and cut you into pieces!"

The cousin was no coward and was quick to take up the challenge. "If it's a fight you want, let's have it!" They punched and wrestled until at last the cousin had the other pinned to the ground. He drew out his knife and held it high, ready to plunge it into his heart.

"Spare me, oh spare me!" he screamed. "I shall give you whatever you ask, if only you will spare my life!"

"If it were me, you would stab me to death without mercy. But you may buy your life back if you wish, for one thousand baht!"

"If one thousand is not enough, you can have two or three!" He was prepared to give him all his father's silver.

"Shut your mouth, blabbermouth! Half your father's silver for your life." That settled, he followed his cousin triumphantly back to her house.

The girl's father greeted his nephew with affection, but he was puzzled. "Nephew," he said, "you have followed my daughter home as her betrothed, but she is already betrothed."

"That is up to her," he replied. So then they recounted the events of the day.

The girl's father listened in silence. "Let me think it over. I shall tell you in the morning whether I consider it appropriate or not." No one slept that night but in the morning her father announced, "Nephew, I am happy for you to be my daughter's husband!" So they were married within the week.

The days after the harvest were relaxing days; people went down to the river to fish, or to hunt for barking deer at night; it was a time to spin cotton and to weave cloth; to build new houses or repair old ones; or to work the elephants in the jungle.

It was also a time for weddings. Dae Birng's cousin was to be married to a young maiden from a distant village and the gongs and drums and cymbals sounded all day and night for days.

On the morning of the wedding, visitors from everywhere flocked to the village to share in the festivities and the whisky drinking, and the boy's father killed two pigs which were cut up and stewed with vegetables and fragrant herbs.

During the marriage ceremony the wrists of the young couple were bound with cotton thread—to ensure their health, happiness, and long life—and they shared a cup of rice whisky with all their friends; and then there was the wedding feast. It was an occasion for much merriment and fun. Some of the visitors had stories to tell and Yuay Birng asked for a story about hunting.

THE FAMOUS HUNTER

There was once a poor man whose wife was very large with child. One morning they went out to gather mushrooms for dinner. They picked a large basketful and were returning home feeling very pleased when they heard a rustling in the bushes. To their horror a savage brown bear shambled onto their path.

They both froze in terror. Then the man flung his spear into the ground for his wife and fled like the wind. The poor woman was too slow and cumbersome to follow, so she grabbed the spear and hurled it at the bear. The bear died instantly. Trembling with relief she called weakly, "My husband, you can come back now. The bear is dead."

The man crept back to the path and saw with amazement that his wife had indeed slain the bear. When he saw what a fine beast it was, he said, "My wife, you are indeed very clever. But would you mind if I said it was I who killed the bear?"

The woman agreed and they chopped up the meat together, carried it home, and traded for rice what they could not eat. The villagers were most impressed.

When the last of the bear was eaten, the man decided to take his wife hunting, to try their luck a second time. On this occasion they tracked down a wild buffalo. But again the man panicked and fled, leaving his wife to slaughter the beast alone. Again they said it was he who had killed the buffalo, and again the villagers were impressed. On a third occasion they met a wild elephant which the woman slew in the same manner. Her husband became known for miles around as the "Hunter of Renown".

As the months passed the green rice covering the hillsides began to ripen, ready for harvesting. The ripe grain attracted birds, monkeys, bears, and even tigers to feed on it. Indeed, a man-eating tiger was seen lurking around the villages; this created great fear among the people. Villagers came to the man, as the Hunter of Renown, and begged him to rid them of the tiger.

How could he refuse? On the appointed day he went, knees knocking and teeth rattling in fright, to the house where the tiger had been prowling. He set his spear in the ground at the bottom of the ladder and climbed into the rafters to wait, hiding away in a pair of baskets.

As dusk fell, the tiger crept up to the house. The man shook with terror at the sight. The tiger sprang onto the verandah and padded inside. As the tiger approached, the man shook and SHOOK! He shook so much that his baskets fell apart and tumbled with him to the floor, just where the tiger was standing. The tiger was so surprised that it fled from the house in one great leap, landing right on the spear which the man had set at the foot of the ladder! He was a hero. All the villagers sang his praises.

Such was the poor man's fame that the bravest men for miles longed to match their skills with his and a duel was arranged for anyone who wished to participate. The morning dawned and warriors arrived from everywhere, with swords gleaming in the sunshine and horses sleek and groomed. Trembling at the very sight of the warriors, our hunter climbed a tree and hid himself. No sooner had he climbed up among the branches than he tumbled in his fright right out of the tree. He landed on a horse which galloped off in a panic. With his sword clutched tightly in his hand he beheaded everyone he passed! That was enough. No one dared to challenge him further. Respectfully they let him be.

Everyone laughed and laughed; even Yuay Birng chuckled, although it was not the kind of story he had hoped for. It was late and dark by then so, one by one, people picked out a lighted brand and stumbled off merrily into the night.

 AFTERWORD

We left Dong Luang in our second wet season, twenty seven years ago. But Peter has kept in touch. Amazingly little has changed: these days one goes by four-wheel drive right into the village instead of walking for five hours from the highway, and strong, timber houses replace the thatched, split bamboo houses of wealthier villagers; otherwise, the way of life seems untouched as people rotate, clear, and cultivate their swiddens as Karen have done for centuries.

The greatest change is in the people themselves. Many of the faces depicted in these photographs have not survived. Uae Birng is among many who died well before their time. Cang died soon after we left, and Maang Diing Phaw took his own life just a few years ago. Diing Kang was shot when he interfered in opium dealing. The fun loving Yuay Birng is currently addicted to opium, like his father before him, as is Sa Saw, the handsome dreamer who married Chii Duay. But Long Tuu and Maw Saw have survived, as have Chii Duay, Pri Birng, Mirng Mirng, and Gaw Birng. Muu Mirng, Muu Lii, and Muu Naang have all grown old.

Life in the hills is back-breaking, hard work. If people can manage to elude death, they will possibly opt for the softening haze of opium addiction. Those who retain their love of life intact are survivors indeed.

 HISTORICAL SKETCH

The Pwo Karen have lived in the Dong Luang area since the early years of the nineteenth century, when they first began to trickle across from Burma, escaping the effects of war between Burma and Thailand. Little is known of their earlier past, however, as they themselves have left no written accounts, and they are mentioned only occasionally in the pre-colonial chronicles of the Siamese and Burmese courts.

They are believed by some to have lived in Burma even longer than the Burmese themselves, since the eleventh century B.C. when Karen first left Tibet to join the Mon in Burma. But it is impossible to prove such theories.

What can be said is that Karen have moved—reluctantly, and in piecemeal fashion, not in great waves—to various destinations, at various times, in search of peace and a stable livelihood; and as they have moved, they have evolved into several distinct groups. The two largest groups are the Sgaw Karen and the Pwo Karen who speak different dialects but are otherwise very similar. All groups have remained "Karen" in essential respects, but they also vary to such an extent that it is difficult to speak of a "typical Karen".

Generally speaking, the Pwo originally settled in the Burmese river valleys and it is interesting to find reference to this lifestyle in the story "Lazybones", as well as in travelers' tales recorded by Theodore Stern. Gradually they were forced back into the mountains where they are today one of the largest minority groups of both Burma and Thailand, numbering about 2.5 million in all.

From time to time Karen are mentioned in other people's histories. From the twelfth century on, they paid heavy taxes to the princes of both Burma and Thailand for forest products and teak. These taxes were collected by government officials whose unpopularity is well documented in the stories of Dong Luang. We also hear of large numbers of Sgaw Karen (but not Pwo) being converted to Christianity in the nineteenth century, of others becoming Buddhist, and of Karen loyalty to the British in World War II. In particular we hear of the long and bitter Karen struggle with the Burmese—since 1948 when Burma was granted independence from Britain—for their own Karen state, Kawthoolay.

The villagers of Dong Luang were not part of the Karen struggle for Kawthoolay; nor were they Christian, nor completely Buddhist. But like their ancestors centuries ago they still grew their rice in swiddens and, like their ancestors, they still adhered to the old spirit traditions, paying respect throughout the year to the spirits of nature which inhabited the mountains, streams, and forests. They believed that life should be conducted harmoniously, and with grace, or the displeasure of the spirits would be experienced in ill health and famine, conditions only too familiar to all Karen. Their way of life would seem to have an enduring viability.

# FURTHER READING

Little has been written about the Karen which is not academic in nature or difficult to find. One of the few exceptions is a well-illustrated book by Paul and Elaine Lewis, *Peoples of the Golden Triangle* (London: Thames and Hudson, 1984). This book is useful because it places the Karen in the context of the other peoples of the hills. Another exception is a book with a different perspective: Jonathan Falla's *True Love and Bartholomew* (Cambridge: Cambridge University Press, 1991). The strange title of this work comes from the names of two Karen who, unlike the people of Dong Luang, are Christian. They belong to the Karen National Defense Organization (KNDO) which has been fighting the Burmese for their independent state of Kawthoolay since 1948. Falla worked as a nurse with the KNDO for a year and this book recounts his experiences.

Burma, where most Karen live, was a British colony from the late nineteenth century until 1948, and the Karen are the subject of several books written about this era. Three worth mentioning are D. M. Smeaton's *The Loyal Karens of Burma* (London: Kegan Paul and Trench, 1887); A. R. MacMahon's *The Karen of the Golden Chersonese* (London: Harrison, 1876), and Ian Morrison's *Grandfather Longlegs: Life and Gallant Death of Major H. P. Seagrim* (London: Faber and Faber, 1946). The latter describes the exploits of Major Seagrim who helped organize the Karen to fight the Japanese during World War II.

American Baptist missionaries were active amongst the Sgaw Karen from the 1830s. They have left some accounts of Karen life and ways. The best of these is Henry I. Marshall's *The Karen People of Burma: A Study in Anthropology and*

Ethnology (Columbus: Ohio University Press, 1922). A collection of Karen stories, some of which are similar to those in this book, appears in Edward Harris's *Way Away Tales* (Philadelphia: Judson Press, 1940).

One who has researched Karen history is Ron Renard, whose paper "The Role of the Karens in Thai Society During the Early Bangkok Period 1782–1873", (in *Contributions to Asian Studies*, vol. 14, 1980, pp. 15–28) is informative. Theodore Stern is another writer who has examined Karen history. His paper "Ariya and the Golden Book: A Millenarian Buddhist Sect Among the Karen" (in the *Journal of Asian Studies,* vol. 27, 1968, pp. 297–328) is a fascinating account of how the arrival of the missionaries sparked millenial revolts by Karen in Burma.

Part of the difficulty of writing a history of the Karen is that their culture varies from place to place and also over time. This makes it very difficult to identify the essence of "Karen-ness". This question is explored in Charles F. Keyes's edited collection of papers *Ethnic Adaptation and Identity: The Karen on the Thai Frontier with Burma* (Philadelphia: Institute for the Study of Human Issues, 1979). See also Gehan Wijeyewardene's *Ethnic Groups Across National Boundaries in Mainland South East Asia* (Singapore: Institute for Southeast Asian Studies, 1990) and Peter Hinton's "Do the Karen Really Exist?" in Wanat Bhruksasri and John McKinnon, eds., *Highlanders of Thailand* (Kuala Lumpur: Oxford University Press, 1983). A recent account that places the Karen experience in the context of the turbulent recent history of Burma is Bertil Lintner's *Burma in Revolt: Opium and Insurgency Since 1948* (Chiang Mai: Silkworm Books, updated 1999).

Finally, here is a selection of papers we have published about the Karen of Dong Luang: E. M. Hinton, "The Dress of the Pwo Karen of North Thailand" (*Journal of the Siam Society*, vol. 62, 1974); Peter Hinton, "Why the Karen do not Grow Opium" (*Ethnology,* vol. 22, 1983) and Peter Hinton, "Matrifocal Cult Groups and the Distribution of Resources Amongst the Pwo Karen", in Paul Cohen and Gehan Wijeyewardene, eds., "Spirit Cults and the Position of Women in North Thailand" *Mankind*, Special Issue no. 3, vol. 14, 1984).

P.H.